The Usborne
Sticker
Picture Atlas
of the World

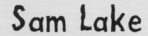

Sam Lake

Illustrated by Nathalie Ragondet

Designed by Samantha Barrett

with Brenda Cole

Contents

The world

The world is divided into seven large areas of land called continents and five large areas of sea called oceans. The picture maps in this book show amazing animals, places and people from around the world.

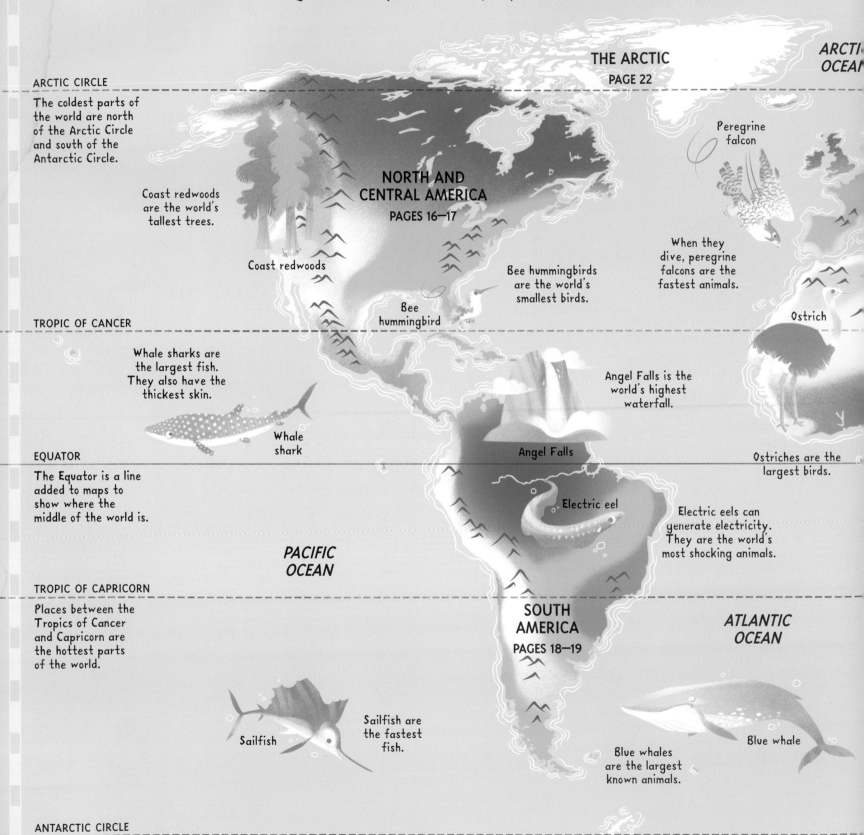

THE ARCTIC
PAGE 22

ARCTIC OCEAN

ARCTIC CIRCLE

The coldest parts of the world are north of the Arctic Circle and south of the Antarctic Circle.

Peregrine falcon

Coast redwoods are the world's tallest trees.

NORTH AND CENTRAL AMERICA
PAGES 16—17

When they dive, peregrine falcons are the fastest animals.

Coast redwoods

Bee hummingbirds are the world's smallest birds.

Bee hummingbird

Ostrich

TROPIC OF CANCER

Whale sharks are the largest fish. They also have the thickest skin.

Angel Falls is the world's highest waterfall.

Whale shark

Angel Falls

EQUATOR

The Equator is a line added to maps to show where the middle of the world is.

Electric eel

Electric eels can generate electricity. They are the world's most shocking animals.

Ostriches are the largest birds.

PACIFIC OCEAN

TROPIC OF CAPRICORN

Places between the Tropics of Cancer and Capricorn are the hottest parts of the world.

SOUTH AMERICA
PAGES 18—19

ATLANTIC OCEAN

Sailfish

Sailfish are the fastest fish.

Blue whales are the largest known animals.

Blue whale

ANTARCTIC CIRCLE

SOUTHERN OCEAN

This map shows world record holders, from some of the tallest, smallest and fastest animals to the highest mountain and the longest train line.

The Trans-Siberian is the longest train line. It goes from Moscow in Europe to the Sea of Japan in Asia.

Trans-Siberian Railway

EUROPE
PAGES 4—7

ASIA
PAGES 12—15

The Great Wall of China

The Great Wall of China is the world's longest wall.

Bar-tailed godwits

Bar-tailed godwits can fly greater distances without stopping than any other birds.

Mount Everest is the highest mountain.

Mount Everest

The sting of the sea wasp box jellyfish can kill a human, making it one of the world's deadliest animals.

Sea wasp

AFRICA
PAGES 8—11

Giraffes are the tallest land animals.

Giraffe

Rafflesias are the world's largest flowers.

The Great Barrier Reef

Cheetah

Rafflesia

The fastest land animal is the cheetah.

INDIAN OCEAN

Dung beetle

The Great Barrier Reef is the world's largest living structure.

One of the strongest insects is the male dung beetle.

AUSTRALASIA AND OCEANIA
PAGES 20—21

Antarctica is the coldest place on Earth.

Scientist

ANTARCTICA
PAGE 23

Western Europe

ARCTIC OCEAN

Cross-country skiers

ARCTIC CIRCLE

European otter

NORWEGIAN SEA

SWEDEN

STOCKHOLM

Midsummer dancers

BALTIC SEA

Traditional painted wooden horse

Fjord horse

NORWAY

OSLO

Stave church

Little Mermaid statue

COPENHAGEN

DENMARK

Mute swan

Western Europe is shown in pink on this world map.

NORTH SEA

SHETLAND ISLANDS

FAROE ISLANDS (DENMARK)

ORKNEY ISLANDS

Angel of the North

Bagpipe player

Porpoise

ICELAND

Geyser

Geysers are jets of hot water and steam that erupt from the ground high into the sky.

REYKJAVIK

European Robin

UNITED KINGDOM

Dolbadarn Castle

DUBLIN

IRELAND

Irish dancer

Cod

Basking shark

POLAND

White-tailed eagle

Wild boar with piglet

Puppet show

BERLIN ■
Brandenburg Gate

SLOVAKIA

HUNGARY

SERBIA

MONTENEGRO

KOSOVO

ALBANIA

Croatian guard

BOSNIA AND HERZEGOVINA

PRAGUE ■
CZECH REPUBLIC

VIENNA ■

AUSTRIA

LJUBLJANA ■
SLOVENIA

CROATIA

Edelweiss flowers

SAN MARINO

St. Peter's Cathedral

Mount Etna is the tallest active volcano in Europe.

SICILY

Mount Etna

MALTA ■ VALLETTA

AMSTERDAM ■

THE HAGUE ■

BELGIUM
BRUSSELS ■

European Union headquarters

LUXEMBOURG
LUXEMBOURG ■

GERMANY

RHINE RIVER

VADUZ ■
SWITZERLAND
BERN ■ LIECHTENSTEIN
THE ALPS

Leaning Tower of Pisa

Alpine marmot

ITALY

ROME ■
VATICAN CITY

Eiffel Tower

CORSICA

MONACO

SARDINIA

Olives

MEDITERRANEAN SEA

LONDON ■

PARIS ■

FRANCE

Camembert cheese

Tour de France cycle rally

Lavender

THE PYRENEES
ANDORRA LA VELLA ■
ANDORRA

BALEARIC ISLANDS

Tower Bridge

The Eden Project

BAY OF BISCAY

Sagrada Familia Church in Barcelona

N
E
S
W

ATLANTIC OCEAN

Bullfighter with bull

MADRID ■
SPAIN

Flamenco dancer

Oranges

Belém Tower

PORTUGAL

LISBON ■

AFRICA

Eastern Europe

Wild mushrooms

Blooms are wild microscopic plants that create bright patterns in the sea.

Eurasian wolves

Sable

Combine harvester

Wheat

URAL MOUNTAINS

Ural owl

Dacha (summer house)

Faberge eggs are jewel-covered ornaments. The fanciest eggs were made 100 years ago for the last Russian emperors.

VOLGA RIVER

ARCTIC OCEAN

Man fishing in ice

The Russian blue is prized for its silver-blue coat, which feels thick and soft.

Gymnast

Faberge eggs

Moscow

Russian blue cat

RUSSIA

Famous Russian ballets include *The Nutcracker*, *The Firebird*, and *Swan Lake*.

BARENTS SEA

Blooms are clouds of microscopic plants that create bright patterns in the sea.

Sea bloom

ARCTIC CIRCLE

Sparrowhawk

The Winter Palace in St. Petersburg

Ballet dancers

Santa Claus's post office

FINLAND

Sauna

Seto woman

HELSINKI ■

TALLINN ■

ESTONIA

RIGA ■ LATVIA

LITHUANIA

SWEDEN

Elk

Walled city of Visby

BALTIC SEA

Balalaika player

CASPIAN SEA

The Motherland Calls statue in Volgograd

Samovar

Dwarf hamster

Sturgeon

Sturgeon eggs are used to make a luxury food called caviar.

ASIA

Eastern Europe is shown in pink on this world map.

Samovars are used to heat water, mostly to make tea.

Cossack dancer

POLAND

WARSAW ■

Cave of legendary Wawel dragon in Krakow

European bison

SLOVAKIA

BRATISLAVA ■

HUNGARY

BUDAPEST ■

Chain bridge

Kiev Monastery of the Caves

DNIEPER RIVER

UKRAINE

KIEV ■

Borscht soup

MOLDOVA

CHISINAU ■

BLACK SEA

Radio telescope

Varna prehistoric cemetery

Whirling Dervish

TURKEY

Only this western part of Turkey belongs to Europe. The rest is in Asia.

CROATIA

ZAGREB ■

BOSNIA AND HERZEGOVINA

SARAJEVO ■

SERBIA

BELGRADE ■

ROMANIA

BUCHAREST ■

Bran Castle

DANUBE RIVER

SOFIA ■

BULGARIA

MONTENEGRO

PODGORICA ■

KOSOVO

PRISTINA ■

SKOPJE ■

MACEDONIA

ALBANIA

TIRANA ■

GREECE

Ancient Parthenon temple

ATHENS ■

CRETE

Dancers in traditional costumes

Northern Africa

EUROPE

MEDITERRANEAN SEA

Moroccan tea set

MADEIRA (PORTUGAL)

RABAT ■

■ ALGIERS

■ TUNIS

ATLANTIC OCEAN

ATLAS MOUNTAINS

TUNISIA

Fennec fox

CANARY ISLANDS (SPAIN)

Sintir player

MOROCCO

■ TRIPOLI

ALGERIA

Cobra

■ LAÁYOUNE

Berber camp

Spice merchant

WESTERN SAHARA

LIBYA

Locust

SAHARA DESERT

Prehistoric rock art

Desert truck

MAURITANIA

Tuareg man

NIGER

NOUAKCHOTT ■

Martial eagle

MALI

Camel train

Gazelle

SENEGAL

NIGER RIVER

DAKAR ■

The Great Mosque of Djenné

NIAMEY ■

BANJUL ■

THE GAMBIA

BAMAKO ■

BURKINA FASO

N'DJAMENA ■

BISSAU ■

OUAGADOUGOU ■

Baboon

GUINEA-BISSAU

GUINEA

BENIN

NIGERIA

GHANA

TOGO

CONAKRY ■

IVORY COAST

ABUJA ■

FREETOWN ■

Woman with bananas

SIERRA LEONE

PORTO-NOVO ■

Traditional mud house

YAMOUSSOUKRO ■

LOMÉ ■

Pangolins are also called scaly anteaters.

MONROVIA ■

Elmina castle

ACCRA ■

Pangolin

CAMEROON

LIBERIA

■ YAOUNDÉ

MALABO ■

EQUATORIAL GUINEA

EQUATOR

CONG

GABON

Seagrass
meadow

The pyramids of Giza are around 4,500 years old. Inside each pyramid is a chamber where a king of ancient Egypt was buried.

Northern Africa is shown in pink on this world map.

ASIA

Oil well

Pyramids of Giza

EGYPT

■ CAIRO

NILE RIVER

RED SEA

Jackal

Felucca boat

TROPIC OF CANCER

Scorpion

N
W   E
S

CHAD

NUBIAN DESERT

Gerbil

Crocodile

SUDAN

■ KHARTOUM

ERITREA

■ ASMARA

Date palms

Tamarind fruit is used to make sauces and sweets.

Church of St. George

DJIBOUTI

■ DJIBOUTI

Tamarind

ADDIS ABABA
■

SOMALIA

Chameleon

Karo people

ETHIOPIA

CENTRAL AFRICAN REPUBLIC

SOUTH SUDAN

Antelope

Somali bee-eater

■ BANGUI

■ JUBA

The Karo people often decorate themselves with body paint.

INDIAN OCEAN

DEMOCRATIC REPUBLIC OF THE CONGO

African elephant with calf

UGANDA

KENYA

■ MOGADISHU

9

Southern Africa

CENTRAL AFRICAN REPUBLIC

CAMEROON

Lovebirds

EQUATORIAL GUINEA

SÃO TOMÉ AND PRINCIPE

LIBREVILLE ■

CONGO

CONGO RIVER

Common octopus

GABON

Mandrill

Chimpanzee sanctuary

BRAZZAVILLE ■

■ KINSHASA

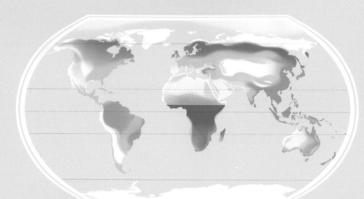

An octopus can change its appearance to blend in with its surroundings.

LUANDA ■

Rhinoceros and calf

ANGOLA

Southern Africa is shown in pink on this world map.

ATLANTIC OCEAN

Hyena

Yellowfin tuna

Hippopotomus

Hammerhead shark

Prehistoric rock carvings

NAMIBIA

Cargo ship

WINDHOEK ■

Meerkat and pup

Portuguese man-of-war

The Portuguese man-of-war has venomous tentacles that can grow up to 50m (165ft) long.

Diamond mining ship

Table Mountai

CAPE TOWN ■

An adult male mountain gorilla is called a 'silverback' because of the silver hair on his back and hips.

SOUTH SUDAN

Coffee beans

ETHIOPIA

SOMALIA

UGANDA

KAMPALA

KENYA

Maasai man in traditional dress

Gorilla

NAIROBI

EQUATOR

Pitcher plants trap and digest insects in their cup-shaped leaves.

Pitcher plant

DEMOCRATIC REPUBLIC OF THE CONGO

KIGALI
RWANDA

BUJUMBURA
BURUNDI

Mount Kilimanjaro

DODOMA

DAR ES SALAAM

SEYCHELLES

Dugong

Lion

TANZANIA

Safari tour

MALAWI

INDIAN OCEAN

ZAMBIA

LILONGWE

Vulture

MORONI

COMOROS

The seeds of the vanilla orchid are used in baking and perfume making.

Zebra

LUSAKA

MOZAMBIQUE

Vanilla orchid

ZAMBEZI RIVER

HARARE

Diver

MADAGASCAR

Victoria Falls

ZIMBABWE

ANTANANARIVO

Great Zimbabwe

Wildebeest

MAURITIUS

PORT LOUIS

BOTSWANA

These are the ruins of a city that was abandoned 600 years ago.

RÉUNION (FRANCE)

GABORONE

TROPIC OF CAPRICORN

PRETORIA (TSHWANE)

MAPUTO

Giant clam

LOBAMBA MBABANE

Ring-tailed lemur

SWAZILAND

BLOEMFONTEIN

Stingray

MASERU
LESOTHO

UTH RICA

Oranges

Cape petrel

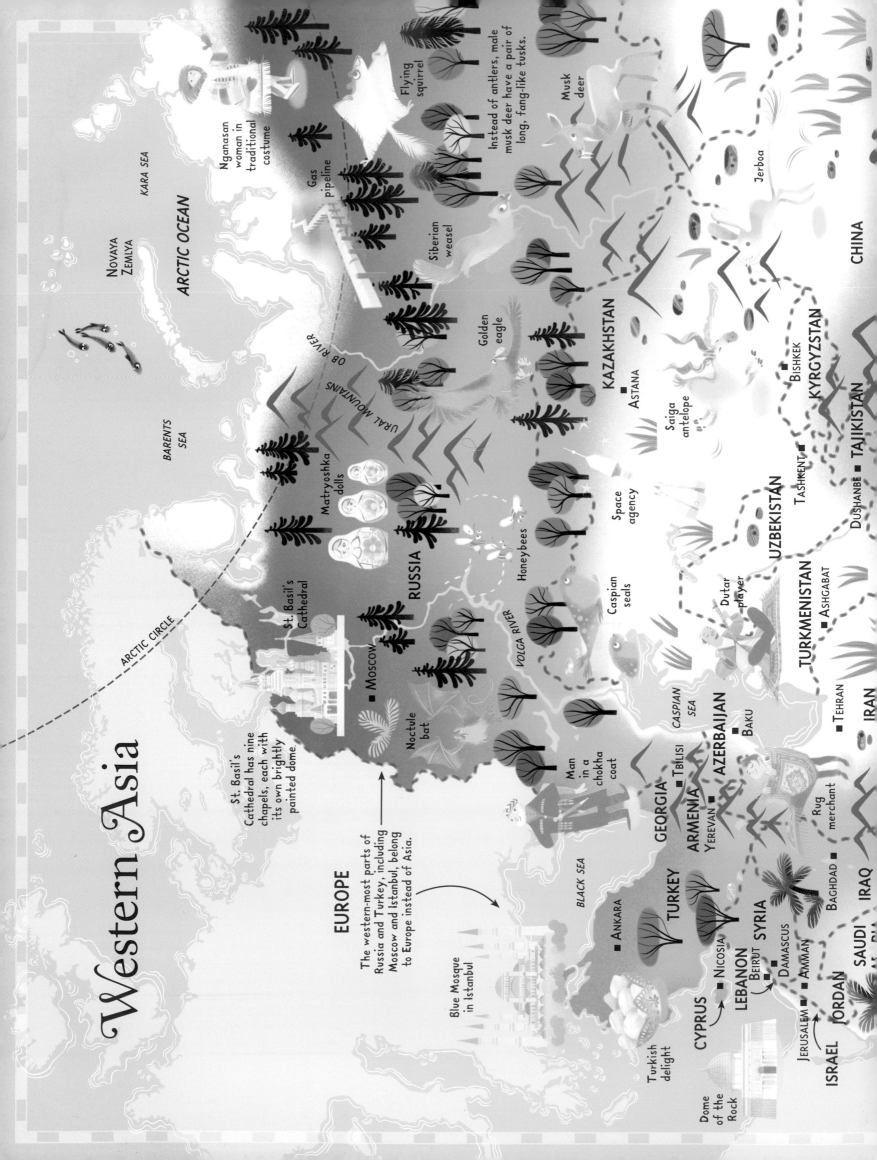

Western Asia

KARA SEA

NOVAYA ZEMLYA

ARCTIC OCEAN

BARENTS SEA

Nganasan woman in traditional costume

Gas pipeline

Flying squirrel

Musk deer

Instead of antlers, male musk deer have a pair of long, fang-like tusks.

Jerboa

Siberian weasel

OB RIVER

URAL MOUNTAINS

Golden eagle

KAZAKHSTAN

■ ASTANA

Saiga antelope

CHINA

Matryoshka dolls

St. Basil's Cathedral

St. Basil's Cathedral has nine chapels, each with its own brightly painted dome.

■ Moscow

RUSSIA

Honeybees

Space agency

Caspian seals

■ BISHKEK

KYRGYZSTAN

UZBEKISTAN

TASHKENT ■

TAJIKISTAN

DUSHANBE ■

ARCTIC CIRCLE

Noctule bat

VOLGA RIVER

Dutar player

TURKMENISTAN

ASHGABAT ■

EUROPE

The western-most parts of Russia and Turkey, including Moscow and Istanbul, belong to Europe instead of Asia.

Man in a chokha coat

Rug merchant

CASPIAN SEA

TEHRAN ■

IRAN

BLACK SEA

GEORGIA

TBILISI ■

AZERBAIJAN

BAKU ■

ARMENIA

YEREVAN ■

TURKEY

ANKARA ■

Blue Mosque in Istanbul

SYRIA

DAMASCUS ■

IRAQ

BAGHDAD ■

SAUDI

Turkish delight

CYPRUS

NICOSIA ■

LEBANON

BEIRUT ■

AMMAN ■

JORDAN

Dome of the Rock

JERUSALEM ■

ISRAEL

TROPIC OF CANCER

THE HIMALAYAS

Tibetan monk

Mount Everest

BURMA

BHUTAN

NEPAL

Red panda

BANGLADESH

GANGES RIVER

BAY OF BENGAL

Bengal tiger

The lotus is the national flower of India. It's used in traditional medicine and cooking.

AFGHANISTAN

Afghan hound

Taj Mahal

PAKISTAN

ISLAMABAD

Girl in a sari

New Delhi

Lotus flower

INDIA

Rickshaw

TAXI

Tea

INDUS RIVER

Ruins of ancient Persepolis

SRI JAYEWARDENEPURA KOTTE

Colombo   SRI LANKA

Sea snakes have flat, paddle-shaped tails that help them to swim.

MUSCAT

Arabian Gulf sea snake

ARABIAN SEA

MALÉ

MALDIVES

KUWAIT

BAHRAIN

QATAR

DOHA

Abu Dhabi

UNITED ARAB EMIRATES

OMAN

Tiger shark

Sawfish

Oil drilling rig

RIYADH

Arabian horse

Arabian dhow boats

Socotra

INDIAN OCEAN

The Kaaba in Mecca

SANA'A   YEMEN

RED SEA

AFRICA

EQUATOR

N
E
S
W

Western Asia is shown in pink on this world map

Eastern Asia

PACIFIC OCEAN

Humpback whale

Puffer fish

Crane

Cherry blossom tree

Bullet train

BERING SEA

Brown bear

Ringed seal

SEA OF OKHOTSK

JAPAN

■ Tokyo

ARCTIC CIRCLE

Russian Orthodox cathedral

Sumo wrestler

NORTH KOREA

■ Pyongyang

■ Seoul

SOUTH

The Forbidden City was the private home of emperors for almost 500 years.

WRANGEL ISLAND

Tai chi expert

EAST SIBERIAN SEA

NEW SIBERIAN ISLANDS

Snow geese

Siberian tigers

Forbidden City

BEIJING ■

SEVERNAYA ZEMLYA

LAPTEV SEA

LENA RIVER

Putorana Plateau

RUSSIA

Buryat girl in traditional costume

■ ULAN BATOR

KARA SEA

Siberian chipmunk

Sayano– Shushenskaya dam

LAKE BAIKAL

MONGOLIA

Ger (tent)

NOVAYA ZEMLYA

YENISEY RIVER

Bactrian camel

GOBI DESERT

KAZAKHSTAN

Man with a fur hat

The Sayano– Shushenskaya dam is the largest power plant in Russia.

Rice bowl with chopsticks

Eastern Asia is shown in pink on this world map.

EAST CHINA SEA

YANGTZE RIVER

YELLOW

CHINA

Panda

Yak

Snow leopard

THE HIMALAYAS

Mount Everest

Pagoda

Hong Kong

TAIWAN

SOUTH CHINA SEA

PHILIPPINE SEA

Pineapples

Nose flute player

PHILIPPINES

MANILA

Junk boat

VIETNAM

HANOI

LAOS

VIENTIANE

MEKONG RIVER

CAMBODIA

PHNOM PENH

THAILAND

BANGKOK

Great Buddha statue

Floating market

ANDAMAN ISLANDS

NICOBAR ISLANDS

NEPAL

KATHMANDU

THIMPHU

BHUTAN

BANGLADESH

DHAKA

BURMA (MYANMAR)

NAYPYIDAW

RANGOON

BAY OF BENGAL

IRRAWADDY RIVER

INDIA

Man riding an Indian elephant

SRI LANKA

Petronas Towers

MALAYSIA

KUALA LUMPUR

PUTRAJAYA

SINGAPORE

The Sumatran rhinoceros is covered in long, reddish-brown hair.

Sumatran rhinoceros

SUMATRA

JAVA

JAKARTA

INDONESIA

Borobudur Temple

Orangutan

BRUNEI

BORNEO

CELEBES

Tarsier

Cowrie shells

NEW GUINEA

Cowrie shells are used to make beautiful beads and necklaces.

ARAFURA SEA

EAST TIMOR

DILI

Komodo dragon

EQUATOR

AUSTRALASIA AND OCEANIA

N
S
E
W

North and Central America

ARCTIC CIRCLE

GREENLAND

Nuuk

Inuit fisherman

Labrador dog

Snowy owl

Maple tree

Igloo

Harp seal pup

Beluga whale

Skunk

Arctic tern

Arctic wolf

Mounted policeman

Grizzly bear and cub

CANADA

Icebreaker

An icebreaker ship uses its sturdy hull to break through ice-covered water.

Husky dogs and sled

Ice hockey player

ROCKY MOUNTAINS

Lumberjack (forester)

YUKON RIVER

Traditional carved pole

Polar bear

ARCTIC OCEAN

ALASKA (USA)

Killer whale

Walrus

BERING SEA

Killer whales hunt in groups, like wolf packs, so they're nicknamed 'the wolves of the sea'.

Golden Gate Bridge in San Francisco

Jumbo jet

A jumbo jet is so big it can carry over 400 passengers.

PACIFIC OCEAN

Common dolphins

The Grand Canyon

Bald eagle

American bison

···RI RIVER

GREAT LAKES

Hopi dancer

Donkey

TROPIC OF CANCER

RIO GRANDE RIVER

Monarch butterfly

Mexican musician

Mexico City ■
MEXICO

UNITED STATES OF AMERICA

American football player

MISSISSIPPI RIVER

The White House

Alligator

Mayan temple

Guatemala City ■
GUATEMALA

San Salvador ■
EL SALVADOR

■ WASHINGTON DC

HAVANA ■

BELIZE
■ Belmopan

HONDURAS
■ TEGUCIGALPA

NICARAGUA
■ MANAGUA

■ San José
COSTA RICA

Howler monkey

The Statue of Liberty in New York

The Statue of Liberty was given to the USA by France in 1886 as a symbol of friendship.

ATLANTIC OCEAN

Space Center

THE BAHAMAS

DOMINICAN REPUBLIC

PUERTO RICO (USA)

HAITI

■ CUBA

JAMAICA

Reggae musician

CARIBBEAN SEA

PANAMA

■ Panama City

SOUTH AMERICA

North and Central America are shown in pink on this world map.

N
W — E
S

South America

CARIBBEAN
SEA

Hawksbill
turtle

**NORTH AND
CENTRAL
AMERICA**

Maracas have been
used in Colombian
music for over
1,500 years.

Maracas

Peccaries

■ QUITO

ECUADOR

Llama

■ LIMA

Machu Picchu is
a mountain city
built 600 years
ago by people
known as Incas.

Machu Picchu

Boy in a
poncho

COLOMBIA

■ BOGOTÁ

VENEZUELA

■ CARACAS

Angel
Falls

Oil platform

Poison dart
frog

Spectacled bear

BOLIVIA

LA PAZ

Spider
monkey

AMAZON RIVER

Blue morpho
butterfly

GUYANA

■ GEORGETOWN

SURINAME

■ PARAMARIBO

**FRENCH
GUIANA**

■ CAYENNE

Rocket
base

Great white sharks
can sense blood in the
water up to 5km
(3 miles) away.

Great white
shark

Sloth

Cocoa beans are used to
make chocolate. They
come from the seed pods
of the cacao tree.

Cocoa pods

River dolphin

AMAZON
RAINFOREST

BRAZIL

Jaguar

Anaconda

Orchid

Gemstone
mining

Capoeira
experts

Scarlet
macaws

Brasilia
Cathedral

■ BRASILIA

EQUATOR

Statue of Christ the Redeemer in Rio de Janeiro

Carnival dancer

Rio carnival is an annual street festival where people dress up in bright costumes and dance.

ATLANTIC OCEAN

Humpback anglerfish

Queen triggerfish

Giant anteater

Caiman

URUGUAY

■ MONTEVIDEO

PARAGUAY

ASUNCIÓN ■

ARGENTINA

BUENOS AIRES ■

Albatrosses have larger wingspans than any other bird.

Albatrosses

South America is shown in pink on this world map.

FALKLAND ISLANDS (UK)

THE ANDES MOUNTAINS

ATACAMA DESERT

Tango dancers

Gaucho (cowboy)

Armadillo

Magellan penguin

CAPE HORN

CHILE

SANTIAGO ■

Monkey puzzle tree

Fur seal

Rockhopper penguins

Flamingos

PACIFIC OCEAN

Opah

TROPIC OF CAPRICORN

N

E

S

W

Australasia and Oceania

NORTHERN MARIANA ISLANDS (USA)

GUAM (USA)

The Mariana Trench is found far underwater. It is the deepest place in the world.

PALIKIR ■

KOROR ■

The Mariana Trench

Lionfish

PALAU

FEDERATED STATES OF MICRONESIA

ASIA

Sacred house

Clown fish

NEW GUINEA

PAPUA NEW GUINEA

■ PORT MORESBY

HONIARA ■

INDIAN OCEAN

ARAFURA SEA

Funnel-web spider

Great Barrier Reef

CORAL SEA

Kangaroo and joey (baby)

Bottlenose dolphin

Frilled lizard

Platypus

GREAT SANDY DESERT

AUSTRALIA

The didgeridoo is a wind instrument that has been used by native Australians for around 1,500 years.

Didgeridoo player

Uluru (Ayers Rock)

Koala

A koala can sleep for up to 18 hours a day

Flying doctor

Sydney Opera House

GREAT VICTORIA DESERT

DARLING RIVER

Black swan and cygnet

Mining for opals (precious stones)

CANBERRA ■

Emu

MURRAY RIVER

Surfer

TASMANIA (AUSTRALIA)

Tasmanian devil

TASMAN SEA

N E S W

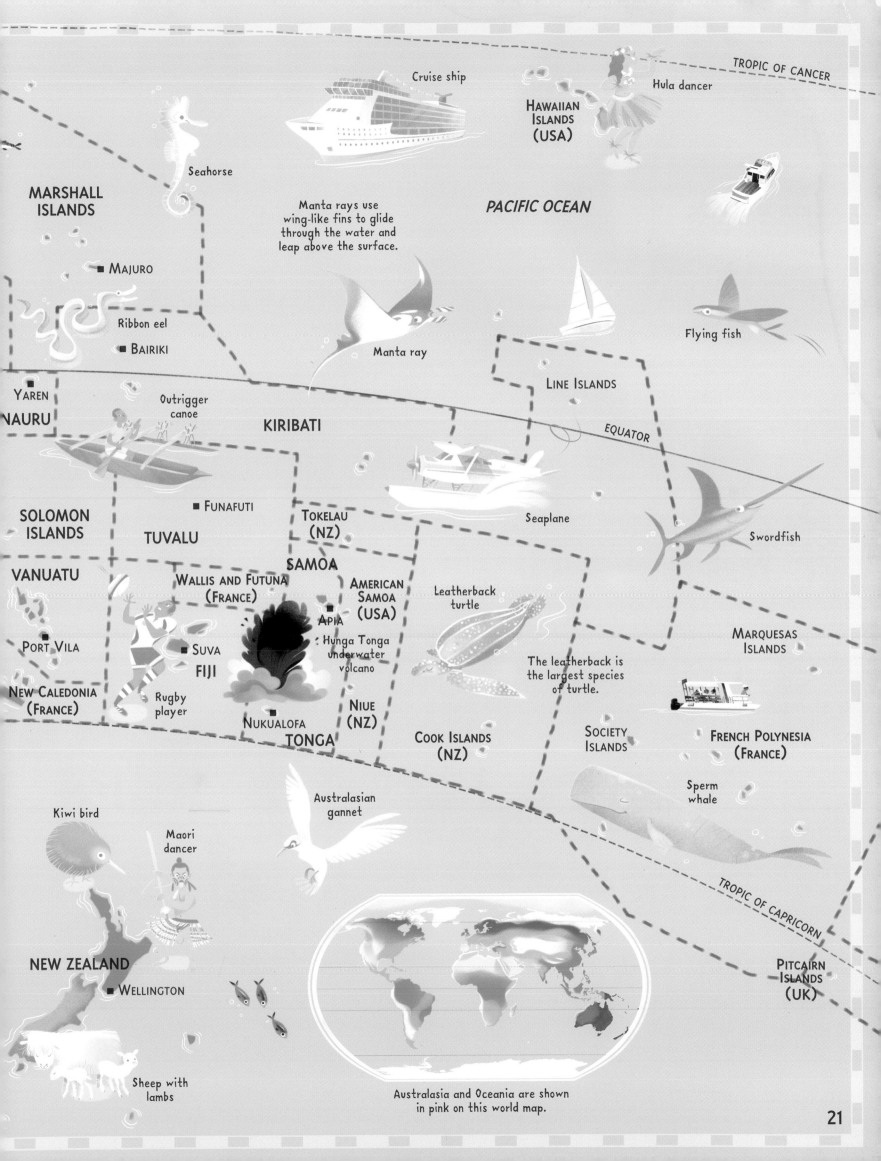

TROPIC OF CANCER

Cruise ship

Hula dancer

HAWAIIAN
ISLANDS
(USA)

Seahorse

MARSHALL
ISLANDS

PACIFIC OCEAN

Manta rays use
wing-like fins to glide
through the water and
leap above the surface.

■ MAJURO

Ribbon eel

■ BAIRIKI

Flying fish

Manta ray

LINE ISLANDS

■ YAREN

Outrigger
canoe

EQUATOR

NAURU

KIRIBATI

Swordfish

■ FUNAFUTI

SOLOMON
ISLANDS

TOKELAU
(NZ)

Seaplane

TUVALU

SAMOA

VANUATU

WALLIS AND FUTUNA
(FRANCE)

AMERICAN
SAMOA
(USA)

Leatherback
turtle

MARQUESAS
ISLANDS

PORT VILA

■ APIA

■ SUVA

· Hunga Tonga
underwater
volcano

FIJI

The leatherback is
the largest species
of turtle.

NEW CALEDONIA
(FRANCE)

Rugby
player

NIUE
(NZ)

SOCIETY
ISLANDS

FRENCH POLYNESIA
(FRANCE)

■ NUKUALOFA

COOK ISLANDS
(NZ)

TONGA

Sperm
whale

Australasian
gannet

Kiwi bird

Maori
dancer

TROPIC OF CAPRICORN

NEW ZEALAND

PITCAIRN
ISLANDS
(UK)

■ WELLINGTON

Sheep with
lambs

Australasia and Oceania are shown
in pink on this world map.

The Arctic

BERING SEA

SEA OF OKHOTSK

GULF OF ALASKA

Chukchi tent

Kamchatka volcanoes

ALASKA (USA)

NORTH AND CENTRAL AMERICA

ARCTIC CIRCLE

ASIA

Lynx

WRANGEL ISLAND

Ptarmigan

CHUKCHI SEA

BEAUFORT SEA

ARCTIC OCEAN

Wolverine

CANADA

Submarine laboratory

NEW SIBERIAN ISLANDS

Ermine

LAPTEV SEA

There is no land at the North Pole, only a thick layer of ice that covers most of the Arctic Ocean.

Musk ox

Arctic hare

Explorer

RUSSIA

SEVERNAYA ZEMLYA

Arctic poppies

ELLESMERE ISLAND

● NORTH POLE

Reindeer with sled

Northern lights

A male narwhal's tusk is longer than an adult human is tall.

KARA SEA

BAFFIN ISLAND

FRANZ JOSEF LAND

Narwhal

Lemming

Fishing village

GREENLAND

Carved figurine

SVALBARD

NOVAYA ZEMLYA

BARENTS SEA

NUUK ■

Woman in traditional costume

Research boat

SWEDEN

Sami people

Puffin

NORWAY

FINLAND

Ice hotel

EUROPE

ICELAND

ATLANTIC OCEAN

22

Antarctica

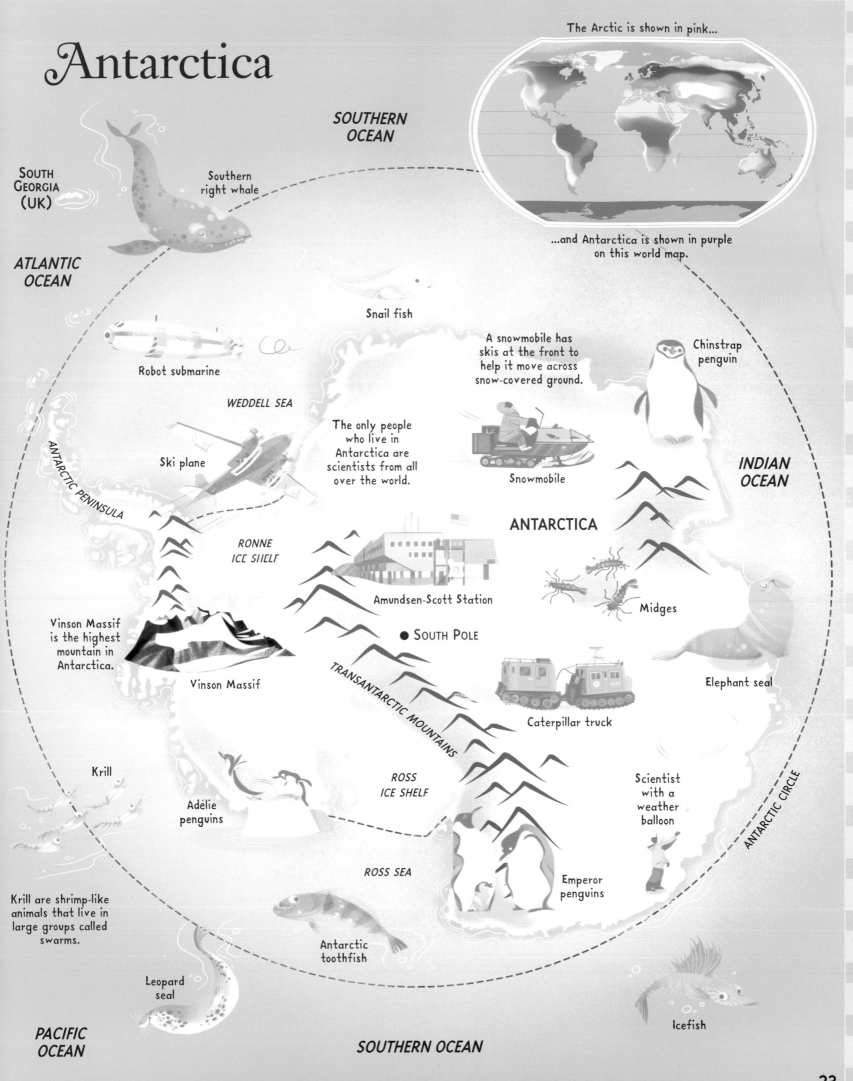

SOUTHERN OCEAN

The Arctic is shown in pink...

...and Antarctica is shown in purple on this world map.

SOUTH GEORGIA (UK)

Southern right whale

ATLANTIC OCEAN

Snail fish

Robot submarine

WEDDELL SEA

A snowmobile has skis at the front to help it move across snow-covered ground.

Chinstrap penguin

Ski plane

The only people who live in Antarctica are scientists from all over the world.

Snowmobile

ANTARCTICA

INDIAN OCEAN

ANTARCTIC PENINSULA

RONNE ICE SHELF

Amundsen-Scott Station

Midges

Vinson Massif is the highest mountain in Antarctica.

Vinson Massif

• SOUTH POLE

Elephant seal

Caterpillar truck

TRANSANTARCTIC MOUNTAINS

Krill

Adélie penguins

ROSS ICE SHELF

Scientist with a weather balloon

ANTARCTIC CIRCLE

ROSS SEA

Emperor penguins

Krill are shrimp-like animals that live in large groups called swarms.

Antarctic toothfish

Leopard seal

Icefish

PACIFIC OCEAN

SOUTHERN OCEAN

23

World quiz

Here are some of the incredible things that can be seen around the world.
Which maps can you find them on? The answers are at the bottom of the page.

Poison dart frog

White-tailed eagle

Chimpanzee sanctuary

Pangolin

European bison

Eiffel Tower

Forbidden City

Taj Mahal

Statue of Liberty

St. Basil's Cathedral

Bactrian camel

Meerkat and pup

Pyramids of Giza

Frilled lizard

The Grand Canyon

Diver

Puffer fish

Outrigger canoe

Southern right whale

Hawksbill turtle

Ringed seal

Inuit fisherman

Arctic poppies

Emperor penguins

Cross-country skiers

For links to websites about places and animals, go to Usborne Quicklinks at **www.usborne.com/quicklinks** and type the keywords "sticker picture atlas".

Digital manipulation by Nick Wakeford

Managing Editor: Ruth Brocklehurst   Managing Designer: Stephen Moncrieff

First published in 2013 by Usborne Publishing Ltd., Usborne House, 83-85 Saffron Hill, London, EC1N 8RT, England. www.usborne.com Copyright © 2013 Usborne Publishing Ltd.
First published in America in 2015. UE.

Answers: Poison dart frog, South America; White-tailed eagle, Western Europe; Chimpanzee sanctuary, Southern Africa; Pangolin, Northern Africa; European bison, Eastern Europe; Eiffel Tower, Western Europe; Forbidden City, Eastern Asia; Taj Mahal, Western Asia; Statue of Liberty, North and Central America; St. Basil's Cathedral, Eastern Europe; Bactrian camel, Eastern Asia; Meerkat and pup, Southern Africa; Pyramids of Giza, Northern Africa; Frilled lizard, Australasia and Oceania; The Grand Canyon, North and Central America; Diver, Southern Africa; Puffer fish, Eastern Asia; Outrigger canoe, Australasia and Oceania; Southern right whale, Antarctica; Hawksbill turtle, South America; Ringed seal, Eastern Asia; Inuit fisherman, North and Central America; Arctic poppies, The Arctic; Emperor penguins, Antarctica; Cross-country skiers, Western Europe.

THE WORLD
PAGES 2-3

Scientist

Blue whale

Peregrine falcon

Cheetah

Sailfish

Coast redwoods

Bar-tailed godwits

Bee hummingbird

Giraffe

Sea wasp

Whale shark

The Great Wall of China

Angel Falls

The Great Barrier Reef

Ostrich

Rafflesia

Trans-Siberian Railway

Electric eel

Dung beetle

Mount Everest

Irish dancer

WESTERN EUROPE
PAGES 4-5

Croatian guard

St. Peter's Cathedral

Oranges

Angel of the North

Midsummer dancers

Cross-country skiers

Traditional painted wooden horse

Geyser

Fjord horse

Flamenco dancer

Sagrada Familia Church in Barcelona

Bullfighter with bull

Eiffel Tower

Bagpipe player

Leaning Tower of Pisa

European Union headquarters